Praise f

"In *An O*w
way to ex
giving the   — a young, curious owl, injured and misplaced, but surrounded by wise council. An intimate quest for knowledge that young readers can relate to."

DAN BAR-EL award-winning author of The Very, Very Far North series

"With crisp writing and strong imagery, Jenna Greene lures readers into the heart of an uncertain fledgling owl on a reluctant journey. Both engaging and irresistible, *An Owl without a Name* expands to illuminate the important service provided by wildlife rehabilitation."

JOAN MARIE GALAT, award-winning author of *Mortimer: Rat Race to Space* and *Too Much Trash: How Litter Is Hurting Animals*

"The wisdom of the owls is a hard-won goal in this coming-of-age story. One misstep sends our feathered hero tumbling into a scary new adventure to discover the power in finding your place in a world where family means more than your name or your home."

ANGELA MISRI, award-winning author of *Pickles vs. the Zombies*

"Both wise and humorous, this big-hearted tale of overcoming self-pity to gain strength in body and spirit is a delightful romp. Fun facts about owls and other birds of prey are woven in seamlessly."

SHELLEY HRDLITSCHKA, co-author (with Rae Schidlo) of *The Grizzlies of Grouse Mountain: The True Adventures of Coola and Grinder*

"Jenna Greene's *An Owl without a Name* is an enjoyable way to introduce children to wildlife rescue and rehabilitation. Along with its charming illustrations by Kimiko Fraser, it not only informs but also inspires empathy as it follows an injured owlet from rescue to release."

GINA MCMURCHY-BARBER, award-winning author of The Jigsaw Puzzle King and Free as a Bird

An Owl without a Name

Jenna Greene
Illustrations by Kimiko Fraser

Copyright © 2023 Jenna Greene

All rights reserved. No part of this publication may be reproduced, stored in a retrieval system, or transmitted in any form or by any means—electronic, mechanical, audio recording, or otherwise—without the written permission of the publisher or a licence from Access Copyright, Toronto, Canada.

Wandering Fox Books, an imprint of
Heritage House Publishing Company Ltd.
heritagehouse.ca

Cataloguing information available from Library and Archives Canada
978-1-77203-463-9 (paperback)
978-1-77203-464-6 (e-book)

Edited by Deborah Froese
Cover and interior book design by Setareh Ashrafologhalai
Cover and interior illustrations by Kimiko Fraser

The interior of this book was produced on 100% post-consumer recycled paper, processed chlorine free, and printed with vegetable-based inks.

Heritage House gratefully acknowledges that the land on which we live and work is within the traditional territories of the Lkwungen (Esquimalt and Songhees), Malahat, Pacheedaht, Scia'new, T'Sou-ke, and W̱SÁNEĆ (Pauquachin, Tsartlip, Tsawout, Tseycum) Peoples.

We acknowledge the financial support of the Government of Canada through the Canada Book Fund (CBF) and the Canada Council for the Arts, and the Province of British Columbia through the British Columbia Arts Council and the Book Publishing Tax Credit.

27 26 25 24 23   1 2 3 4 5

Printed in Canada

*To a lawnmower, a yelp,
an owl, and an idea*

Contents

1. The Fall 1
2. Fight or Flight 8
3. Marble Eyes 13
4. Dr. Millican 18
5. Hazel and Basil 22
6. Restless Wing Syndrome 30
7. Moving Day 34
8. Orientation 38
9. Fledgling 44
10. Sage 49

11	**Attendance** 53
12	**Eagle Eye** 60
13	**Demonstrations** 69
14	**Regiment** 75
15	**Rave** 81
16	**Confrontation** 86
17	**Advice** 90
18	**Home** 94

Author's Note 101

Acknowledgements 103

1
The Fall

FAR BELOW my nest, the humans are using tools to scrape at weeds and make piles of crusted leaves. It's been days since they've emerged from their habitat. Perhaps the warm air and cloud-free sky has tempted them. I hope to alert my sister to the human presence by nudging her with my wing. She doesn't stir from her nap. Not that humans interest her. At least not as much as they interest me. But then, everything interests me. I tend to plague my parents with endless questions:

Why do only some animals have feathers?

Why is our nest in this tree?

When will my flight lessons begin?

How long until I'm full grown?

However, my parents aren't here to address my curiosity right now. They are out seeking breakfast, since Sister and I can't hunt on our own yet. I hope they bring back a tasty morsel. Squirrel is my favourite.

I peer down over the edge of the nest. Perhaps, if I pay close attention, I can learn a few things on my own.

The smallest human runs to the shed and covers her eyes. Her name is Olive. She begins to count, "One... two... three..."

I lean forward. What is she doing?

"... nine, ten. Ready or not, here I come!" she declares before flinging her hands off her face and darting behind the shed.

What human custom is this?

Cautiously, I step over the edge of the nest for a closer look. I catch a glimpse of Olive's hair floating in the breeze. The branch wavers. Leaves stir. I take another step and—

Whoosh!

I lose balance and pitch forward, catching air. I tumble, and the world flip-flops.

"Mother! Father!" I squawk as colours streak by. "Sister!"

The fall is quick, the landing abrupt. My stomach slams into my throat, and something tears at my right wing.

Ouch.

I blink, swivelling my head around. Nothing looks familiar.

I've never been on the ground before. The grass prickles my stomach, and the scent is strong, tickling my nose. I don't like being out in the open. A dog's bark startles me, and I jump, pulling my wing feathers. I wince. My wing is caught in the fence bordering the humans' yard.

The fence is made from stiff grey wire that forms square holes smaller than my head. My left wing feathers are snagged in a hole near the bottom. Though I wiggle and wriggle, I can't pull them free. All I gain is exhaustion.

What should I do? My parents would know, but they aren't here. If Sister noticed my fall, she has no way to help. Not that I hear her call.

I'm alone for the first time since hatching.

I crane my neck upwards until I spot the branch where I live, but leaves hide the nest itself. My stomach rumbles. A slice of meat would fill me up, offer comfort. I could eat a rabbit, a hare, or a vole. Since I'm not picky, I'd settle for a mouse.

Tired, I lay my head on the fence. I'll rest until nightfall. By then it will be cooler, and I'll have more energy to wrestle free. Or my parents will have rescued me.

I drift in and out of sleep. At one point, I waken and reach for my sister's warmth before I remember where I am. I shift, yelping as my wing feathers tug. I resettle and close my eyes, but I'm listening. Awake.

Hours pass and Olive's voice fades away. The sun's shadows reach me, and finally, I slip into a stupour.

Until the horrible sound arrives.

I've heard this whirring sound twice before from my protective perch, while snuggling close to Mother, Father, and Sister. My parents warned me never to go near the machine that makes the horrible sound.

The man—also known as Mr. Miller—rides the machine around and around the yard. With each pass, the grass shortens.

Why?

I do not know. All I *do* know is that I have never liked the horrible machine or its horrible sound. I like it even less today when it's so close. My ears hurt. I can't keep my beak from clacking as my insides shudder.

Humans have odd habits.

I need to get away! What if its whirring blades get too close to me? What if—?

Mr. Miller yelps, and the horrible machine stops.

He jumps off his contraption. With tentative steps, he approaches my location. When he squints, I know he's spotted me. He creeps closer. He seems so big. I feel small.

Thankfully, he backs away and turns to face the house. "Marie!" he calls. "Olive! Come here!"

The rest of the family is coming? I've never been this close to any of them. I like watching the Millers from my perch, not from the ground.

I attempt to free my wing, grunting with effort.

With her hand joined to her mother's, Olive tiptoes closer.

"Not too close," her father warns. "Stay back."

"Why?" asks Olive.

"You should never approach an injured animal."

"She's hurt?"

She? I'm a boy! Soon to be a man! If my sister heard that—

"What should we do?" Mrs. Miller asks.

"I don't know," Mr. Miller says. "I wonder what's wrong. Do you think she hurt her wing, or is she just stuck?" He pulls a shiny black rectangle from his pocket and points it at me.

Click.

Mr. Miller takes one step nearer, then another, until my finely tuned hearing picks up his heartbeat. Too close. Time to wriggle again. Beak clacking, I yank my wing again and it pinches.

This isn't fun. The day I'm having!

"She's scared!" Olive exclaims before bursting into tears.

Why is the girl crying? I'm the one who should be upset! I'm the one on the ground when I'm meant for the tree. I'm stuck, while she can flail all her hairless limbs. I miss tree bark and leaves. I miss my nest. Security and silence. The moon.

"Mother! Father! Rescue me!" I shriek.

"Okay, okay," says Mrs. Miller. "Let's call someone to help." From her pocket, she pulls out a black rectangle like Mr. Miller's. She taps it in a few spots and then holds it up to her ear. A voice squawks through the device. Mrs. Miller asks a few questions and turns to face me. She cocks her head to the side and stares as though she is sizing me up. Then she lowers her arm and returns the rectangle to her pocket. "Twenty minutes," she says. "Someone from the Birds of Prey Centre is on their way. A man named Christopher. He'll come with special gloves and a cage."

What are those for?

Olive dries her cheeks. "Will they be able to help?"

"I think so, sweetie," Mrs. Miller soothes. "They'll know better than we will."

Clapping her hands, Olive hops.

I do neither, obviously. And not just because I do not have hands. Wings are superior, anyway. I do not know this man they speak of. I've seen gloves before, but I don't know how any pair of gloves could be special. Will they be different than the kind Mr. Miller wears while he rips weeds from around the house? And a cage... I'm not certain what that is.

I doubt I'll like it.

Okay, Operation Freedom is *on*.

Twist. Wiggle. Twist. Wriggle.

2

Fight or Flight

THE FAMILY eats supper under a fledgling elm tree that offers minimal shelter or shade. Their meat is seared and slathered with red and yellow goo. Every few minutes, one of them plucks sliced fruit from a tray and pops it into their mouth.

Mr. and Mrs. Miller don't look at me often, instead opting to eye the path beyond their yard. Olive watches me, though, her small eyes watery. Every so often, she points in my direction or asks a question about me, which her parents attempt to answer. Mostly, they say, "I don't know, sweetie."

Circling my head around, I watch the path too. A road. I think that's what they call it. A place for cars to travel upon. My parents told me that when I'm able to fly, I'll have to avoid roads. A collision with a car could be fatal. Knowing that one approaches now, especially one that does not belong to the Millers, makes me nervous.

Christopher, they'd said, would bring special gloves and a cage. I shudder. I'm not sure I want to find out what that means.

While the family munches their food, I resume wriggling. I try to free myself once more, ignoring the pain and torn feathers because I'm determined. I am a mighty owl!

Gravel crunches down the road. He's coming!

I wince, and with a furious twist and wrenching of feathers, my right wing pops free of the fence.

Freedom!

I don't waste time glancing at the arriving vehicle. It's time to escape and try my first flight. Expanding my wings, I—

Ouch! Owie!

Okay, flying is out. Too many lost feathers and an aching wing bone. Instead, I hop. Sort of. It's more of a waddle. A waddle-hop. I keep tilting to the side. How awkward! I nearly stagger into some thistles.

Something stomps behind me, paired with clicks and a foreign coo. As the sounds grow louder, I hop faster. Hands approach, covered in extra-long, heavy gloves. Special gloves? They smooth down my body, catching my legs and pinning them together before lifting me.

I'm in the air, but not in the way I want to be.

I swivel my head around. The man—who I assume is Christopher—has a yellow hat that hides most of his forehead. His eyes are the same colour as my talons. His face moves too close. Hot breath stirs my feathers. The sight of big teeth unnerve me. I squirm. My body shifts, but not my legs. His grip, though not painful, is uncomfortable. Tight.

The Millers approach, slowly. I'm not sure if they are disinterested or relieved. Human eyes are small. They don't express much emotion.

Mr. Miller hangs back while Mrs. Miller continues forward, holding Olive's hand.

Olive brushes a tear aside. "Can I pet the owl?" she asks Chirstopher.

Pet? What does that word mean?

Christopher's yellow hat shakes from left to right. "No," he says gently. "We don't pet wild animals, even those as cute as this little one. We don't want them to get used to human contact because our goal is to release them back into the wild once they heal from their injury."

Olive looks disappointed, but I am relieved. Being so close to humans is new. I've observed them before, sure, and all their odd mannerisms, but such closeness is overwhelming.

A sweet smell lingers in the air. It drifts from Olive's pink mouth which is missing several teeth.

"We could name her 'Althea,'" Mrs. Miller suggests. "That's a dignified name."

My ears perk. A name? For me? I've only been called "Brother" before. Or "Little One," the same thing my parents call Sister.

Mr. Miller looks at me thoughtfully. "Assuming it's a girl."

"Actually, this owl is a male." This comes from Christopher. "Females are larger than the males."

If my sister hears that, she'll be laughing.

"Snowy," Mr. Miller states. "He's a Snowy Owl. Look at all that white on him."

I don't think that's right. My chest may be white, but it won't be for long. Soon my feathers will darken to match my parents.

"That's not right," Christopher says.

Ha. I knew it.

"The white is his baby fur. Down," Christopher continues. "He's lost a lot of it already, and the rest will fade soon."

"He's a baby?" Mrs. Miller's voice trembles slightly.

"Born just a bit ago," Christopher confirms. "I'd estimate a month. But owls grow quicker than humans. He's nearly full grown."

"He must miss his mother," Mrs. Miller whispers.

Indeed. And my father. And even my sister.

Mr. Miller grunts. "So, not 'Snowy' then?"

"Call him 'Snowy,'" Olive insists. "Snowy."

Christopher nods. "That sounds like a fine name to me. He's a Great Horned Owl, by the way."

"He has no horns," Olive points out.

"No, he doesn't," all three adults agree in unison.

Christopher raises a finger above my head. "But he'll get ear tufts soon."

"Okay." Olive's eyebrows pop up. "What now?"

Mrs. Miller kneels so she is eye to eye with little Olive. "Christopher will take him to the Birds of Prey Centre, where a vet will check him over. Do you remember what a veterinarian is?"

"Someone who takes care of animals."

"That's right." Mrs. Miller's lips turn upward. "Snowy will be well cared for. And we can visit him soon. We just have to say goodbye to him for now."

"Okay, Mom."

Christopher shifts me from one hand to the other, but I barely notice the transition. I'm focused on the word, *goodbye*. I'm being taken away. I don't know where, but I'm going somewhere new. I'm not supposed to be going anywhere! I should be with my parents and sister, safe in my nest. Something has gone terribly wrong.

I don't know the Millers well, but at least they are familiar. If they leave, or if I leave them...

I don't like this. I don't like this at all.

I clack my beak in fear.

3
Marble Eyes

AFTER FAREWELLS are cheerily exchanged—by the humans, not by me—I'm carried to a blue truck with four doors. One door pops open and on the seat is a box-like thing with thin metal bars running horizontally and vertically on one side, like a gate. A thin towel pads the inside. Christopher unlatches the barred side and places me in the box. Then he closes the latch with a muted *click*. I nudge the latch with my head, but it holds fast.

There's a slam, a slight rocking, then the truck rumbles to life. An abrupt shift tosses me to the side. After that, the ride is gentle. Corners are taken slowly. We ease in and out of faster and slower speeds.

Being enclosed makes my chest tighten. This is far different from my nest. It isn't enjoyable. There may be holes for me to peer through, but there isn't much to see. Colours and shapes blur before me, and the air sifting in through the holes is stale.

Drowsy, I allow my eyelids to droop. My beak clacking slows.

There's a mild screech and a sudden lurch. My eyes pop open. I'm here. Somewhere new on an adventure I didn't sign up for.

The truck door opens. Then I'm lifted, box and all. Jostled up and down, I flop over. There's barely enough room to right myself—especially with my sore left wing, but somehow, I manage. I peer through the holes, spying a blur of green. We're marching past various species of trees.

My box passes through a door, and the scenery changes. The trees disappear. Cream colours coat everything. Then movement stops, and my box abruptly lowers. I bounce upon landing.

Nothing seems to happen for a while, at least from my limited view. I nudge at the box lid again. It still doesn't budge. I'm waiting for something, but I don't know what, nor do I know if it will be good or bad. Trying to still my beak clacks is impossible.

When the box finally does open, I blink furiously, trying to adjust to the bright light above me.

"Well, hello, Marble Eyes," a voice coos.

Marble Eyes? Is that me?

What's marble?

A face comes into view. Soft features are paired with long hair. The girl isn't a grown adult, as far as I can tell, but she isn't far from it, either.

"I'm Halle," she says.

I'm... *nobody*. Well, I'm somebody. But who?

I don't have a name. Just *Brother*. Or *Snowy*, the name that little Olive gave me. I never needed more than that in my nest. Now that I'm no longer in my nest, who I am and what I should be called feel important.

Bending to peer at something written on the side of my box, Halle exclaims, "Snowy! Well, nice to meet you. I suppose it is an appropriate name."

I guess Christopher must have written down the name the Millers gave me. Still, I would prefer another.

"You still have some of your pale down. Someone thought you were a Snowy Owl, I presume?"

It's not like I can answer her.

Swinging my head left to right, I peer at my new surroundings. The room is narrow and plain with walls similar in colour to my feathers. My box settles on a cluttered table beside another box, an open one. Next to the door, there is a sink.

"You're alright, Marble Eyes." Halle links her gloved hand around my feet, tugging them close. She carries me to the sink. "I'm still in training, but I do know what I'm doing. Let's clean you up and check you over. Dr. Millican will be here in the morning."

Positioned in the sink, warm water runs over my body. The sensation is unfamiliar, but enjoyable. A white substance is rubbed into my feathers, then rinsed away, leaving a faint smell of something new but not unpleasant. Once the water is turned off, I shiver. Halle wraps a pale pink towel around me, with only my head peeking out. She raises me out of the sink, hugging me close to her body. I twist my head back to the sink. Dirt and a few downy feathers cover the bottom of it.

I'm transported back to the table, next to my box, and patted down with the pink towel. When I'm dry, Halle removes the towel completely and tucks me back into the box. Smiling, she pokes my beak once, drawing her hand back quickly, then winks at me.

"You're a kind fellow, right?"

I'd like to think so.

"This must all be very strange to you."

You have no idea.

"You're all clean. There's a small tear on your left wing, but Dr. Millican will fix that right up. Trust me, I've seen worse injuries."

So perhaps other young owls have been through this trial.

"Life happens, with a few bumps along the way," Halle continues. "Sometimes you fly into a window. Other times a tree falls down—with you in it. The good news is there's always a person around to help you after. It'll work out, as long as you accept the hand that's trying to feed you, right?"

Not fully understanding what she means, I bob my body and swivel my head for another glance at my surroundings. My beak clacks twice.

The door starts to close on my box. Is this my new home?

"See you later, alligator." Halle's smile is the last sight I see.

I'm an owl, not an alligator. Birds and reptiles have few similarities. This girl is not very intelligent.

4

Dr. Millican

HALLE IS young and uses odd expressions. Dr. Millican is an older man with strong arms and wise eyes. I like the girl better. She bathed me, instead of raising my wings repeatedly like Dr. Millican does. Halle didn't prod my belly or poke a silver-stabber through my feathers and into my body. The pinch from Dr. Millican's weapon is brief, but not fun.

Soon after Dr. Millican lays the silver-stabber down, I begin to feel odd. I can barely keep my eyes open. Should I sleep some more?

I sleep, but I don't realize it until I wake up. My injured wing is wrapped in white material. Movement is tricky for that wing, easy for the other. How am I supposed to learn to fly like this?

Halle said Dr. Millican would help me.

With my beak clacking incessantly and my feathers trembling, I'm transported past the sink again. Dr. Millican sets me onto a metal slab with odd symbols on it. I consider waddling away, but hesitate, watching the symbols spin and finally settle.

A moment later, I'm scooped up. "You're a good weight for a young guy," Dr. Millican announces.

Wait for what?

"Your wing will heal soon. Trust me, I've seen worse injuries. That should make you feel good, huh?"

Why would that make me feel good? This man is strange.

Placing me in the sink, Dr. Millican steps back to assess me. He tilts his head to one side. Without meaning to, I imitate him. When he shifts angles, I do too. A noise at the door causes him to look to the left, leaning backwards slightly for a better view. Heart fluttering, I mimic his move again, but I don't have to lean back. My head turns farther than his does.

Dr. Millican turns back to me. "Show-off." His lips turn up into a smile.

What does he mean by that? I turn my head to the other side, stretching it as far as it will go.

Dr. Millican claps his hands. "Well done. One of the perks of being an owl."

Or a disadvantage of being a human. They don't seem to be able to spin their heads, and they can't fly, either. How well do they see at night? How fine is their hearing? I suppose their longer legs are an advantage, but flight is superior. Not that I know, of course, as I've never flown. However, seeing my parents fly is a majestic sight. I can't wait to try it. Soaring above the treetops, swooping down on prey...

I sigh and fluff my feathers. Hopefully, my wing will be released from the white fabric soon so I can try. Then I can find my way home, back to my family.

My beak clacks. What if I never go home? What if I never have the chance to fly? Would I still be a bird? Or would it make me something else?

Dr. Millican's voice interrupts my thoughts. "So, what shall we call you?"

Snowy? That's what the Millers decided. And that's what Halle read on the side of my box. Of course, Halle also called me "Marble Eyes." Still not sure what that means.

Without looking at the box, Dr. Millican declares, "Looks like no one named you yet. Of course, whatever name we give you is our gift to you, but we can only guess what you'd like to hear. No one knows how you refer to yourself in your head." He scratches his chin before mumbling, "I sound like Halle. Been spending too much time with her. Being a veterinarian is different from being an animal philosopher, huh?"

I don't know what a philosopher is, but sure. I will agree.

Leaning close, Dr. Millican peers at me with eyes much smaller and dimmer than mine. Definitely not owl eyes. "You have an intelligence, that's for certain," he says. "You might not know the same things humans do. You might know far less, or far more." Straightening, Dr. Millican wraps gloved fingers around my legs and transports me back to my box.

Here? Again? If this is my new home, it needs some improvements. Foliage. The light touch of wind. A nest lined with soft bedding. I miss my tree, my parents' calls, and Sister's body pressed against mine. Sadness creeps under my feathers.

"In a while, crocodile." Dr. Millican waves as he settles the lid on the box.

Crocodile? That's even worse than alligator! For a man who works with animals, he needs to study more.

5
Hazel and Basil

MY STOMACH growls. Ignoring the pangs, I close my eyes. Sunshine leaks through the window. Dawn. The best time for sleep.

The door opens, and Halle appears. The light switches on. Brilliant white light floods from the ceiling. While I'm grateful that Halle brings food, I blink rapidly, annoyed that my rest has been interrupted by all this brightness. I prefer stars to sunshine.

"Hi, Marble Eyes."

Hello.

She holds a bowl with slices of savoury meat. Dangling them above me, she slips them into my eager beak one at a time.

Sated, I close my beak.

"You're going to have roommates for a short time. Is that okay?"

How should I know?

Using his back to brace the door, Dr. Millican enters the room carrying a box half the size of mine. "Make way!"

Through the barred side of my box I have a good view as my "roommates" are revealed.

Inside the smaller container are two half-owls. I mean short. Little, but fully formed. Tilting my head, I wonder how they can be so small. I could step on these critters. Their beaks are like mine, dark yellow. Just like mine, their eyes are bright. Both have white eyebrows and a patch of the same on their chins. Miniature wings have white spotting on brown feathers.

"Meet Hazel and Basil," Halle announces. "Fellow owls."

If you say so.

Dr. Millican does a quick inspection of both creatures. He raises their wings and tests the grip of their claws on his hand, whispering in Halle's ear from time to time. Once the owls are back on the table—and not even in their box—both humans exit the room.

One of the maybe-owls shoots a glance in my direction. "Hi!"

I nod.

The other bobs up and down. "Hello."

I nod again.

"What's your name?" the first asks.

"I don't know."

"You don't know your name?" they ask in unison.

"Well, I have been called a few..."

"Ah." One of the maybe-owls clacks their beak. "I understand. They call me Hazel..."

I start to reply. "Nice to meet—"

"...but I call myself Basil."

"Oh," I say.

The other maybe-owl chimes in. "They call me Basil."

"That's—"

"But I prefer the name Hazel."

I blink several times. My beak clacks. Confusion ruffles my feathers. "I don't understand."

The maybe-owls hop forward, perfectly synchronized. Soon they are beside my box, peeking in through the holes. I rise up to peer over the edge. Backing away three steps, they glance up at me. "Hi!" they repeat.

"Hi. Er... are you owls?"

Basil hops on the spot. "What do we look like?"

"Sort of like owls. Just really small."

"Burrowing Owls," Hazel says. "We're Burrowing Owls. You might call us tiny, but we are bigger than mice."

"And frogs," Basil adds. "And snakes, though they are longer, of course. Larger than gophers, you know. And—"

"Okay. I understand." I don't need any more animal comparisons. Clearly, this pair are owls. I've just never seen any so small. But again, there is a lot I haven't seen yet. There's a lot I still need to learn.

Hazel hops. "We are brother and sister."

"That's nice."

"Do you have a sister?" Basil asks. "This is mine."

"I do have one. I don't know where she is right now."

Basil bobs his head. "Are you one of those nest owls?"

Nest owls?

Hazel adds, "You live in a tree, right?"

"Doesn't everyone?"

Hazel and Basil stare at each other, then at me. Several seconds pass without either of them blinking. When they do speak, they do so slowly.

"*Nooo*," Hazel says. "We live in burrows. Underground."

"That's why we are called Burrowing Owls," Basil adds. "You've never heard of Burrowing Owls?"

"No."

"Wow. You haven't experienced much," Basil says.

"Not really. I was born this spring. Aren't you young, too?"

More staring. Absence of blinks.

"*Nooo*. We've seen four seasons," Hazel says.

"But you're so little."

Feathers ruffling, Basil snaps, "That doesn't mean we're babies. You're big, but new. Size matters as much as names do."

"Okay." This pair confuses me. Perhaps by tomorrow I will understand what they mean.

Hazel struts away, finding a perch on the edge of the counter. "I pretended to have no appetite so Dr. Millican would bring us in—all that for this?"

Moving to comfort his sister, Basil says, "We both pretended. It was worth it. How else would we learn about the new arrival?"

"I didn't need to starve myself to meet a ninny," Hazel says, huffing.

Puffing out my chest, I declare, "I'm not a ninny." Not that I know what a ninny is.

Hazel glances back. "Well, you don't know much."

"Not yet. I'm learning."

Basil and Hazel prance back, hopping in unison. "What have you learned?"

My thoughts flee.

"Uh-huh. Smart guy." Basil tucks his head against his chest. "I'm taking a nap. Wake me when Dr. Millican comes back, Hazel."

Hazel nuzzles her brother until he dozes off. Once he is asleep, she struts back over to my box. "You never said your name."

"Oh."

"That's not an answer."

"I . . . I don't know my name."

"Make one up," Hazel suggests.

"I don't think . . ." My beak clacks. For some reason, I peek behind me. "Can I do that?"

"Why not?"

"Doesn't someone else name me?"

Hazel nods. "They can. But that doesn't mean you have to accept it. Remember, Halle and Dr. Millican call me 'Basil.'"

"How do I choose a name?"

"Pick something you like."

"So, I could choose Snowy or Marble Eyes," I slowly respond. "Or Brother."

"Do you like those?"

"I don't know."

"Then they probably aren't right for you."

This is aggravating. "I'll have to think of one on my own then."

"Would you like some suggestions?" Hazel leans forward, eyes eager. "Brutus? Agamemnon? Phillipe?"

"Those don't—"

"Tippy? Sandalwood? Excelsior? Hezekiah? Gandorf?"

"Gandorf? What kind of name is that?"

Hazel ignores me and keeps rambling names I've never heard before. "Thor, Owl of Thunder? Perseus the Sallow? Paris of Snow? Tulip? Theodore? Antony? Aureleus? Benedictine? Ornaldine? Flor—"

"No!" My head twitches. Those names are horrendous.

Hazel blinks. "Hmm. Maybe Sage will know a perfect name for you."

"Who is Sage?"

"Sage is—"

A clatter from the hallway interrupts Hazel. Then Halle pushes through the door holding a tray. Eyeing the contents, Hazel squeaks and Basil awakens. As slices of meat are dangled in front of them, I repeat, "Who is Sage?"

Between bites, Hazel murmurs, "A story for another time."

Restless Wing Syndrome

DAYS ARE simple here. Halle brings food. A circular device on the wall ticks incessantly while a small black line slowly circles past strange symbols, over and over again. A few bits of down fall from my chest. My shoulder gradually begins to twinge less.

I wait. When Halle removes Hazel and Basil, I wait for their curious eyes to return. They do not. I wait for other interesting arrivals, of which there are none. Dr. Millican visits only once, for the briefest moment. He inspects my left wing, removes the bandage, and clucks approvingly as I flap. Then he is gone. I rest in my box, pretending it is a proper nest.

"Hey, buddy," Halle says one day.

Buddy. Could that be my name?

"What are you thinking?"

Owl thoughts. I wonder what *she's* thinking. Maybe she wishes she had feathers.

Sweeping the floor, she whistles an odd tune that sounds like no bird I ever heard. She finds a new song when she scrubs the sink.

After tidying up a few supplies, she turns to study me. I find her glance unsettling.

What is her assessment of me? Am I a disappointment? I was to the Burrowing Owls. Does Halle think I'm a ninny as well?

"You're so cute," she announces before departing.

Cute? *Guh*. Rabbits are cute. I am a mighty predator.

I'm also alone again, and bored. Agitation ripples through my limbs. I stretch my wings, wishing I could fly back to my family. If only I knew how.

I poke at the box with my beak. I nip at the edges, fraying them. When this does nothing to ease the tension inside me, I strut around, thrusting my body against the box's sides as I go. Repeated impact forces it to move, shifting along the length of the counter.

Each impact distracts me. I thump my body harder against the box. It teeters and then tumbles to the ground. It lands sideways, as do I. With some effort, I right myself. Shaking, I slide forward, hesitant. Freedom is new to me. So is the ground. I stretch my neck upward, a vantage point that frightens me. It reminds me of my capture a few weeks ago. A similar sense of vulnerability washes over me. I don't like it. For some reason, I feel more alone here than I do in my box. Oh, how I wish I could fly!

I retreat to the box and huddle in the corner, feet buried under the rumpled towel. My left wing flaps of its own accord, restless. My beak clacks until I duck my head against my chest to soothe myself. Thoughts of Mother and Father—even Sister—float through my mind, again and again.

Home. I want to go home. I'm tired of daily surprises. Where are the bark and insects, leaves and wind? Everything here is sterile. Silent.

The door opens. I jump, eyes growing wide. Shoes approach, those odd things that humans wear on their feet. These ones have laces. They're a shiny silver colour, duller than the material on the sink and counter but striking, nonetheless.

The shoe-wearer ducks down, revealing Halle's familiar features and her lopsided smile.

"How did you get down there, Marble Eyes?" she asks.

Shame for my behaviour washes over me. When Halle reaches into my box to adjust my position, I snap crossly. Without intending to, my beak connects with her skin. She howls, drawing her hand back.

Instantly, I feel bad.

Halle's shoes shuffle away. A moment passes, then water runs. When Halle returns and peers into my box, her eyebrows are pinched.

"You're in a mood," she says.

She lifts the box and settles it back on the counter. I flop over during transport. By the time I'm back on my feet, the door has closed behind her.

My mood sours further. I'm in this situation by my own choice. A bad choice. I leaned out of the tree and fell. I cannot blame anyone else for being here.

A perfect return to my home and family might not be possible, so I change my wish to make the best of where I am. I ask for one thing: for Halle to return. Perhaps I can nuzzle her fingers. Or flap charmingly at her. Or somehow show her that I am sorry.

Moving Day

SLEEP IS supposed to change a foul mood, but it fails to soften mine. Halle's absence gnaws at my soul. I wish I could apologize to her.

When Dr. Millican enters the room, I'm instantly alert. When he takes me out of my box, I let him, without fuss. Placed on the squat metal slab with the strange symbols, I remain in perfect position until I'm shifted again. I am on my best behaviour, even as my wings are raised and inspected.

Dr. Millican's shoulders rise and fall. "I think you're ready. On to better adventures. I'll miss you, Little Guy."

For a moment, I'm overwhelmed. I wonder if *Little Guy* is a suitable title for me. Then I blink. What am I ready for? What adventures await me?

Shaking overtakes me. My beak clacks twice.

Smoothing his gloved hand down my feathers, Dr. Millican whispers, "Hey. You'll be alright. This is just the next stage. I'd love to keep you, but you weren't hurt that badly. Trust me, I've seen cases. Owls and cars... not a pretty sight. Halle will visit you, for certain. You'll make new friends, both owl and human. Rehabilitation is what we're after, not captivity. Keeping you safe for a while is different from keeping you forever."

With an encouraging smile, he says, "You'll be fine." He tucks me back inside my box and closes the lid, diminishing my view.

The familiar feeling of being lifted and carried rolls through me. I don't know where I'm being taken or what will happen once we get there. To calm myself, I tuck my wings tightly to my body, bracing against jostles and bumps. I pinch my beak to keep it from clacking and try to be brave. Maybe I'm being taken home, back where I belong. If so, I want my family to see me at my best. I duck my head to groom myself.

Disappointment ruffles my feathers as I recall Dr. Millican's words. He told me I will meet new owls and other humans. That means I'm not going home.

Will I ever?

The box shifts and I slide to the right. There isn't time to wallow. Centring myself inside the box, I raise my chin and puff out my chest. I'll still want to make a good first impression with whomever I meet.

What will my name be in this new location? Little Guy? Snowy? Marble Eyes? Something else entirely, like Ernesto or Capulet Montague?

I may not be able to find my way home by myself, but Hazel says I can find my name. Only none sound right.

There must be a name for me. If I find one, other things won't seem as bad. What about Snowy Guy? Ernesto Montague?

They don't feel right either.

The transport stops. There's a foreign sound that I can best describe as a creak, similar to the sound the Millers' gate makes when Olive swings it open. My box is settled on the ground and tipped forward slightly. I edge toward the back, my heart pounding. The metal door opens. I slide forward.

Sunshine awaits beyond the box, as does fresh wind. In front of me grow grass and weeds. Branches extend from the stunted trees lining a fence that looks like the one in the Millers' backyard.

"In you go," Dr. Millican says, nudging me forward.

Nope.

There's a soft coo, followed by a shuffle. I jump back into my box as two owls approach. I recognize their scent, even before they emerge from the shadow of their own box. As sunlight strikes them, I note they look like younger versions of my parents. These owls still have a light layer of white down coating their bodies. One has a slice through its left wing. The other walks with a limp. They don't seem intimidating, yet my heart thumps against my ribcage. I don't know whether to be alarmed.

Dr. Millican makes shooing noises and shakes my box until I slide forward. My feet scrabble for purchase. Although my talons are strong, the more the box tilts, the more I slide. Soon, I tumble out. With a swipe, the box disappears behind me. Dr. Millican retreats, swinging a gate closed in his wake, the creak repeating.

My surroundings are new. Again.

The air holds an unfamiliar scent, tangy and sharp, with a hint of juniper. My wings flap open, then snap closed. I wish I knew how to use them properly. I want to be high above, where I feel safe. The wide yellow eyes of my fellow owls stare at me. I focus past them, at the wire that lines the space, each open square smooth and uniform. I'm caged in. There is no retreat. Unless I could gnaw on the wire...

I blink, bringing myself back to awareness. The pair of owls draws nearer, slowing. Their beaks clack, though not as rapidly as mine.

I think I'm supposed to live with them. These are my new friends.

"Hi!" the one with the cut wing says in a cheery tone. "My name is Herbert."

The other owl limps closer. Though the angle of his brow makes him look annoyed, he sounds equally friendly. "It's nice here. No need to be shy. I'm Thomas."

They stare at me expectantly. I gaze back.

"Well?" Thomas prompts. "What's your name?"

My chin drops. That question again? How do I answer? I can't.

Perhaps my name is as unreachable as my family.

8

Orientation

I AM in a habitat. That is what Thomas and Herbert tell me. The wire surrounding us forms the top and sides, keeping us in and others out—which I suppose is good. I can see through it easily, to the similarly sized habits neighbouring us, even to the sky. After a while, I barely notice the wire and stop bumping into it. Once, I rubbed against it to scratch my feathers.

The habitat is comfortable and roomy enough for the three of us. I like the shade provided by the thick branches of the juniper sitting in the centre. It smells familiar, and resting behind the raised roots offers a bit of privacy. If I edge out from under its leaves, I can perch on a smooth rock and warm my body under the uninterrupted rays of sunshine.

Right now, Thomas and Herbert stand side-by-side on the large mound of dirt piled in the corner. I join them. They don't react, so I sidle closer. Herbert coos, shifting toward me until our wings are pressed together. Closing my eyes, I pretend it is Mother or Father beside me, and we are huddled in the nest I was born in. Sister's head is tucked under mine.

Except it isn't the same.

Heart hollow, I give up on my imaginings. Opening my eyes, I ask, "Herbert?"

"Yes?"

"What do you know about your name?"

He stares at me, head cocked. For a moment, I think he's fallen asleep with his eyes open. Without blinking, he eventually turns away, hopping off to find a new place to rest. Predicting the same reaction, I don't bother repeating the question to Thomas.

We are fed twice a day. Halle comes in the morning with fresh water and meat. There are separate bowls for each of us, so sharing isn't a problem. I choose the one on the left. When Halle smiles at me, I wiggle my torso and flap my wings. This is my way of saying "hello."

And "sorry."

Wearing her usual smile, she nods.

In the evenings, when the sun begins to descend, food is brought by a boy named Mussab. His teeth are extra shiny, and his head is wrapped in fabric.

"Rest well," he tells us, taking time to pet each one of us on the head before departing. Mussab doesn't talk as much as Halle, but he is friendly. I like him.

Herbert spends his time out of the sun, nestled underneath the wealth of leaves and branches our tree provides. He's an observer. A listener. His clever eyes track the progress of insects. With equal intensity, he tracks Thomas's actions and mine. Possessing the ability to be still for hours, he is as stable as the tree he rests upon.

Thomas passes the hours either sleeping or strutting. He likes to pace, ascending and descending the mound of dirt in the corner, foraying over the roots. Sometimes he walks the habitat perimeter. As the hours pass, his limp becomes more prominent. It doesn't deter him though. He soldiers on.

From our position on the ground, we take turns eyeing the high branches of the tree. When I look up, I think of my nest, my home. I suspect the others think of theirs too.

Views from the ground hold my interest too. A low fence runs like a barrier between the front of my pen and a gravel pathway. On the other side of the pathway sits a high wooden fence covered with netting. The occasional coo or squawk rings out, so it must be another habitat, though much larger than the one I share with Thomas and Herbert. When the fence gate occasionally swings inward, I catch a glimpse of cut grass. But I pay little attention to this space. More important things draw my attention.

My habitat sits between two others, identical in size. The habitat on the west appears to be empty, but the one on the east houses Hazel and Basil. Their habitat has scraggly trees and a pair of bushes at the top of a dirt slope covered in holes.

"Burrows," Basil tells me one day.

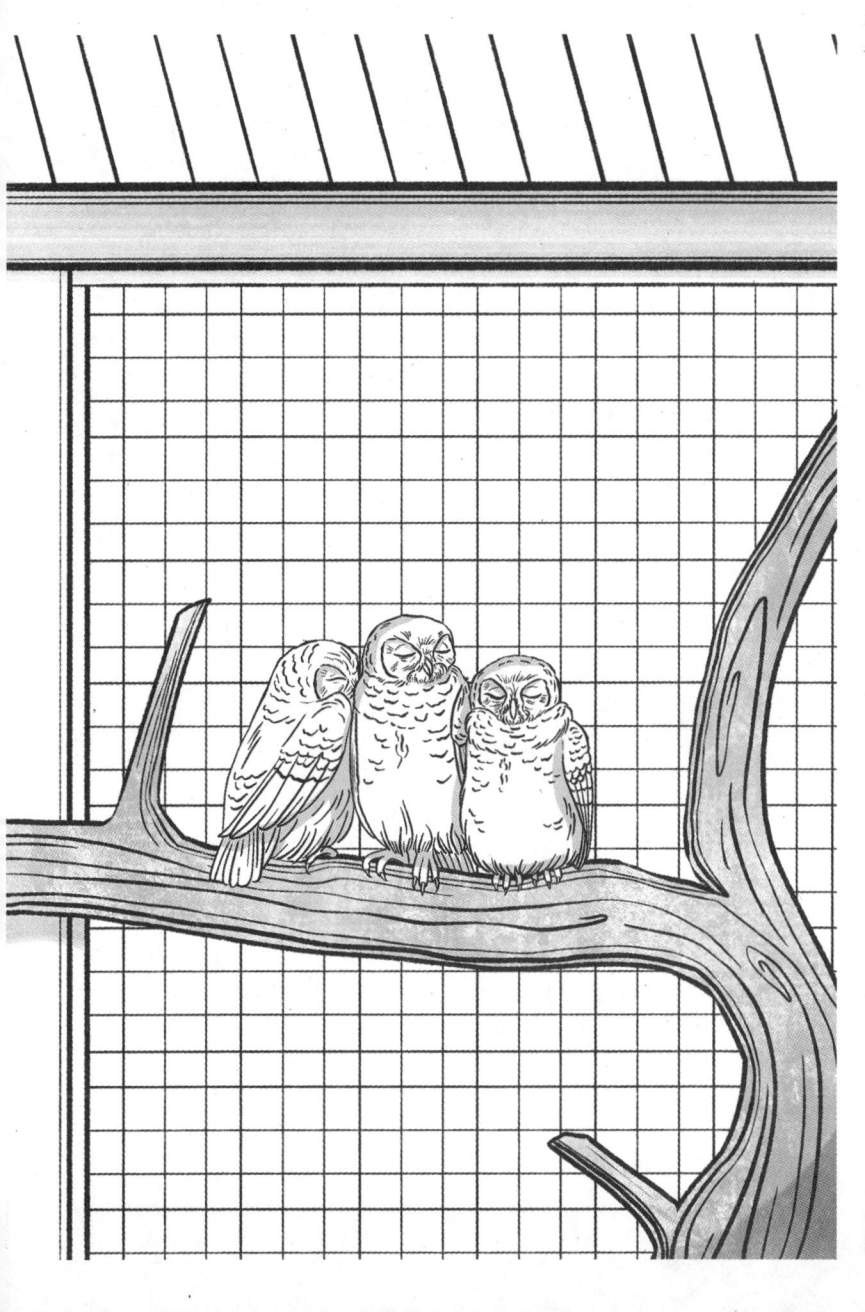

The pair rise with the sun instead of the moon as Thomas, Herbert, and I do. This means I do not encounter Hazel and Basil regularly. At times, their space seems empty, except for starlight. When I do see them, they hop about chasing sunbeams, chattering gaily. Sometimes they seize their supper from Mussab and drag it inside their burrows to feast.

One morning, their antics are too noisy to slumber through. I saunter to their edge of the wire fence and chirp, "Hello."

"Have you found your name yet?" Basil asks.

"I think I have one that suits," I tell them.

"Really?" asks Hazel.

"What is it?" Basil demands.

"Faisel."

They skitter back several inches.

Cocking her head to the side, Hazel says, "Why?"

"It's like yours," I say.

Basil shakes his head. "You can't be like us."

This hurts my feelings. I pout.

"I don't mean it like that," Basil tells me. "A name has to be about you, not about copying your friends."

This both upsets me and elates me. I'm glad to be called a friend. Still, lacking a name makes me sad. "How do I find my name?" I say, as much to myself as to them.

"Talk to Sage," they reply in unison, as if this is an easy task.

Sage. That name again. Who is this Sage? As I open my beak, a shiny beetle skitters across their path. When they chase it, the chance to ask my question has passed.

Turning away from Hazel and Basil, I ignore questioning looks from Thomas and Herbert. They don't yet know about my quest for a name, and I'm not ready to tell them. I want to hide behind one of the roots, but Thomas stands in the middle of them.

I retreat to the west edge of the habitat, as far away as I can get from Hazel and Basil. Nestling near the gate where Halle and Mussab enter, I gaze into the adjoining habitat. While my new home has one tree, the habitat on the west has several trees crowded together, some pine, some spruce. Stillness lurks inside. It reminds me of the emptiness I feel while I search for my name. A name could give me meaning. Purpose. But how do I find one? I have no clues to follow, no path to lead me to salvation.

Sage can help me, they said. Except, who is Sage? A fellow owl? Perhaps. One that I don't know how to find.

Ducking my head, I doze off, thankful to escape from my problems for a while.

9
Fledgling

MY FIFTH habitat day arrives, along with a question from Thomas: "Why don't you try to fly?"

I blink into the first rays of sun as they peek over the horizon. I ask him to repeat the question.

"Fly? Why don't you do it?"

There are many reasons. I eye the wire ceiling of our arena. Space is a concern. Ability is another. With a shudder, I remember my last fall. "I don't know if I can."

"You'll never find out sitting still."

True.

I shift my talons, taking a moment to watch an ant disappear into its hill. "Can you fly?"

"I'm ready to try," Thomas responds.

"Why now?"

"I need a buddy to fly with me. Someone to give me a necessary nudge."

We both turn toward Herbert. Perched at the base of the tree, his head is turned away from us. My gaze flicks to his injured right wing.

"Herbert can't." Thomas' whispers what I'm thinking. "His wing."

"But Dr. Millican—"

"Did his best," Thomas says firmly.

Attempting to fly in front of Herbert is cruel. Resisting the urge is timid. I must choose.

Thomas sidles closer. "Please?"

"Alright." My ability to fly won't ease Herbert's suffering, nor change his fate. "How do we—?"

"We jump." He doesn't sound confident.

"Let's try a small leap first," I suggest.

Thomas unfurls his wings. He backs up a few steps and then rushes at me, head jutting forward. As he nears, his eyes narrow and his beak clacks. He jumps, flapping, and crashes almost instantly. When he rises, his face is marred by dirt. I can't help chuckling.

"You try," he grunts.

I do not bother with the running start. I simply flap my wings, gaining power with each thrust. Winded, I pause. Before Thomas can taunt me, I try again, flapping with every ounce of energy I possess. Longing for a high perch, I release my hold on the ground. Then I bounce against the wire. A screech tears from my mouth on impact, and a loud thud echoes.

As I right myself, Thomas scrambles over. "You did it. You flew!"

I did. Not well, and not for long. Not with any accuracy of direction, but I flew. Using my own power. I celebrate by bouncing my chest against Thomas's chest. Herbert nods grudgingly, longing embedded deep within his eyes. Catching more praise from Thomas, I bow, then whirl, half expecting my parents to embrace me.

They don't.

They aren't here.

Even though I'm not officially alone, I feel as though I am. Heart heavy, I sink and hold my wings tightly against my body. I inch away from Thomas toward the edge of my habitat, resting my head against the west fence. Thomas continues his flight attempts. Whenever he succeeds, he receives a nod from Herbert and a blank stare from me. Bouncing, he applauds himself and continues his efforts, gaining skill and stamina as the hours pass. Branches rustle overhead each time he reaches a new perch.

"One attempt is all you have the mettle for?" asks a foreign voice with a rough timber. Each syllable is enunciated perfectly. This is not Herbert or Thomas. Like me, their words exit at a high pitch.

Has someone new been brought to our habitat? No. Not possible. The door is closed. I look around Hazel and Basil's habitat. The voice isn't coming from there. The owls are in their burrows.

"No answer?"

Whirling toward the voice, I search the west habitat, the one I'd thought empty. At first, neither sound nor motion calls to me. Then, just as I'm about to turn away, a grey blur catches my attention.

A tall owl steps into view. This creature has a large, round, grey face, and hidden ears. A small yellow bill sits in the middle. The owl stares down at me and addresses my stilted flight practice. "Your fellow Great Horned followed the pursuit for much longer than you did."

"Yes. He did," I reply.

"Why?"

"I don't know," I lie. The truth is, I was defeated by the absence of my family.

"Ah. When you do know, perhaps you'll find more answers."

I don't know what this means, so I opt for a greeting. "Hello. Have you just arrived?"

"Hello. No."

"I haven't seen you before."

"No, you haven't," the grey owl replies, "because you look without seeing."

I blink. "How can someone look without seeing?"

"Plenty do."

Okay. I try a new tact. "What kind of owl are you?"

"A Great Grey, I believe."

"I'm a Great Horned."

"Indeed."

"I think you are supposed to ask my name," I say slowly.

"Do you know your name?"

"I—" I swallow. "People call me Snowy or Marble Eyes."

"Is that your name?"

"No." I pause. "What's *your* name?"

"When the wind taunts my aging bones, my name is Ancient One. As my memory fades, Ghost is my title. In moments where the sun strikes my feathers to reveal the colours imbedded within the grey, I am Lucinda, Owl of the North."

"You can be all those things?"

"If I decide. My fate is my own. Correct?"

I'm expected to respond. I'm expected to acknowledge and agree. The words won't release from my throat.

"I am many names, just as I am many things," she continues, eyeing me sidelong.

"What do I call you, then?" I ask.

"Assuming we speak again?" She swiftly softens her brush-off with the words, "To most, I am Sage."

"Sage!" I gasp.

10

Sage

"WHAT'S MY name?" I blurt.

Sage blinks.

"My name. I've been told that you will know my name."

"Told by whom?"

"The Burrowing Owls—Hazel and Basil."

With a nod, Sage says, "That pair. Did they state that I would know your name or that you should ask me about it?"

"I—uh..."

"The first question you should ask is whether you *have* a name."

I shuffle back. It had never occurred to me that I might not possess one. "Do I?"

"By nature of your question, I assume you do."

My brain is sore. Sage's speech is odd, twisted, and confusing.

I try again. "So, what is it?"

"What is what?"

Resisting the urge to sigh, I repeat, "What's my name?"

"Are you asking how your name reflects you, or how you reflect your name?"

"I-I-I don't know." Why couldn't this be easier?

"Why do you seek a name?" Sage asks, bending her head and scratching it with a talon.

"Shouldn't everyone have one?" I counter.

"Indeed."

Was that a yes or a no?

Sage stares. I'm uncomfortable, so I fidget and clack my beak. As seconds pass, I grow still, but my feathers cling to my body and my talons tighten, digging into loose soil. I'm close to something essential. Close to a name. Yet this old owl is holding me back. Unfair! I was told Sage had answers for me. She hints that she has what I seek, yet she seems to have no intention of granting it. "Do you know my name?" I press, grit in my tone.

"Not yet."

"Not yet?"

"No."

Breath slides into my throat through a narrow channel. "When will you know?"

"That is to be determined."

This is ridiculous. I rotate my head, gluing my eyes to the roots of the tree. They are stable. Predictable. But Sage is confusing. She teases me with riddles instead of helping me.

"That's it?" she calls as I retreat. "You have no further commentary?"

"That's it," I repeat.

For the rest of the day, everything falls downward: my posture, my attitude.

After Thomas rests, he renews his flight attempts. With each try, he gains strength. To avoid his path, I sit next to Herbert, hoping to share misery. Unfortunately, Herbert's spirit doesn't match mine. Nodding at each of Thomas' successful dives—only limited by the scope of our habitat—Herbert murmurs praise.

"Why are you not sad?" I ask him, bitterness coating my words.

Herbert tilts his head, a question in his eye.

"Thomas. He's showing off," I say.

"He isn't. There is no malicious intent in his efforts."

Is everyone going to insist on fancy vocabulary today? I haven't the heart for it. Tired, I try again. "Aren't you jealous? He can fly and you can't."

"I might be able to. One day."

I scoff, glaring at his left wing. "Doubtful."

Herbert refuses to join my foul mood. "Sage taught me to focus on what I have instead of what I lack."

My beak twitches. "You've spoken to Sage?"

Chuckling, Herbert nudges me. "Of course. Wisest bird around. And, fortunately, our neighbour. I saw you speaking with her. How lucky. She doesn't always show herself. It has been weeks since we've been able to converse. What did she say? What wisdom did she share?"

"Nothing," I grumble, turning away. Suddenly, the habitat closes in on me. I can't find a space away from Herbert's optimism, Thomas's flights, the Burrowing Owls' cheerfulness, or reminders of Sage.

Nothing.

I have nothing.

Tucking my head under my wing, I hide within myself. Hours pass.

The door clanks. "Suppertime," Mussab announces as he places bowls of meat strips on the ground. He is soon gone.

Herbert and Thomas swoop in to feast, but I decide not to move. Not to eat.

Not to be.

Without a name, I am nothing, so nothing I will be.

11
Attendance

HOT AIR taunts my senses as the humidity rises. Thomas dozes on a high perch. Herbert plops into his water bowl, dousing his feathers with moisture. I hide under a branch. In the slim shadow, I stare at the world past my cage. And it is a cage, not a habitat, this prison that I'm trapped in.

Basil and Hazel do not mind the heat. At least, it doesn't seem to bother them. They flounce around, pecking at each other, scurrying through games of hide-and-seek. Their voices rise high as they call to Sage. She responds with the occasional double hoot and a flap of her wings. Signals. Their easy communication spreads through multiple habitats. It's annoying. I huff, refusing to admit jealousy.

Hazel and Basil were wrong. Sage did not help me find my name. She is a fraud.

As if sensing my mood, the weather changes. Murky clouds roll in. When raindrops begin to land, others seek shelter. The Burrowing Owls retreat to their dens. Herbert and Thomas hide beneath the juniper. I do not hide.

I step into the storm. I welcome it, though my feathers droop with moisture. My body is soon wracked with chills. Now I'm miserable inside and out.

Mussab ducks by in a damp slicker, passing food without staying to socialize. The meat goes untouched.

A subtle sound draws my attention to the west. Sage stands tall and still, canary eyes aimed my direction, half-moons framing them. Her gaze penetrates my soul.

Unashamed, I stare back.

My suffering is her fault. If she knows my name, she should give it to me.

OVER THE next few days, the storm dissipates until only a few showers tiptoe overhead. The sun shines unfettered, and flowers release their blooms.

Mussab and Halle take on new duties, strutting about carrying shoulder bags. Mussab prunes branches and Halle plucks weeds. Both collect dried leaves and place them in the bag. They transport other owls to and fro. Other workers, whom I rarely meet, travel past my view as well.

They are nameless nobodies, just like me.

Whistles and coos draw my attention to the habitat across the path from me, the one with the wooden fence covered in netting. The door is open, wider than ever before, revealing a few pillars with a net strung high above.

"Are there owls in that habitat?" I ask.

Thomas glances over. "You are speaking again?"

How many days have I gone without doing so?

"Opening day nears," Herbert supplies.

"What is opening day?" I ask.

Herbert shrugs.

"How do you know that opening day—whatever it is—is getting closer?" I ask.

Herbert nods at Hazel and Basil as they leap around their territory, playing one of their games. "They told me. They know a lot. They didn't stay still long enough to say what it means, though."

"We could ask Sage," Thomas suggests.

"No." No point in that. Sage holds information in her throat, refusing to share.

THE NEXT day a big change occurs. First, voices arise. Human ones. Excited squeals. Footsteps announce the presence of visitors before they slide into view. They spy Hazel and Basil first.

"They are so little. Cute!"

"Are they really owls?"

The Burrowing Owls hop about, undeterred by an audience, or perhaps encouraged by them.

When the humans approach our habitat, Herbert sidles backward, hiding his scarred wing. Thomas approaches. I remain where I am, partly hidden by shadows.

"What kind of owl is that?" a child asks, pointing at Thomas.

"What do they eat?" asks another.

"Can they really turn their heads all the way around?"

Mussab and Halle try to keep up with the questions. Their answers overlap.

Fingers point.

Countless shiny rectangles aim in our direction. What are those strange things and why do people always have them?

"These are Great Horned Owls," Halle states. "Each are rescues with different injuries, different stories." She tries to point at Herbert, but he ducks away. "That one was attacked by a coyote. He's lucky he survived."

My chest pinches. Poor Herbert!

"They are juveniles?"

"Yes. All three." Mussab nods. "Did you know most Great Horned are born between February and March? Not many people know that owls don't have the best sense of smell. They can hear well, though, sensing prey miles away."

Mussab relates more facts. I learn things about my future: how I will age and when I might reproduce. Likely, I will live thirty years, though I don't know if that's a long time or a short one.

Curiosity piqued, I listen. This is strange, to learn about my life from the mouths of humans.

The day lengthens. My eyelids droop.

"Snowy!"

I jerk. The name "Snowy" is as familiar as the young, sing-song voice calling it.

The Millers stand before me. As Mr. Miller aims his rectangle at me, Olive bounces, trying to tug free from her mother's grip. She wiggles the fingers of her free hand in my direction.

"Hi, Snowy!" Olive cheers, dragging her mother closer.

They are not my family. These are not my parents. Yet they are a connection to home. I shimmy in their direction, anxious for closeness, for the taste of something familiar.

Olive squeals as I approach, glancing at her mother.

"He looks healthy," Mr. Miller comments.

"Healing well," Mrs. Miller agrees.

Olive reaches out a hand, though she cannot touch me because of the barrier running between the path and my pen. I creep closer.

"Snowy!" Olive's smile stretches across her beak-less face. "I'm so proud of you."

I halt.

She is proud?

Of what?

Proud of me for falling from a tree? For enduring the unknown, adjusting to routines? I have accomplished nothing. I have not even discovered my real name.

Abruptly, I turn away, giving the Millers my back.

"Snowy?" Olive's voice is ringed with disappointment. "Mom, he won't look at me."

"I know, Sweetie."

The Millers offer a few more calls before moving on, but I ignore them. Herbert and Thomas stare at me, questions in their eyes.

Following the Millers' departure, the day drags on. More groups of people approach. Sometimes Halle and Mussab are with them. At other times, not.

I hide in the foliage. Invisible.

At twilight, all the guests leave. Mussab delivers our evening meal, talkative for once. "I hear you had special visitors," he says to me. "It must be nice to see friends."

I stare back. I wish I could shrug. Humans can shrug. Of all their odd mannerisms and gestures, this is the only one I find useful.

As the sounds of night welcome me and I settle for the evening—head tucked against my chest—Sage's voice reaches out to me. "You wasted a moment."

Reluctantly, I turn. It doesn't take long to locate her. Her eyes blink at me from between the branches of the tree she perches in. "What?"

"You wasted a moment. The reunion with your family."

"They aren't *my* family."

"They could be, just as Thomas and Herbert could be your family. As much as the world could be. You must seize the moment when it appears."

"What are you talking about?" My words escape as a growl.

Sage shakes her head. "You are ridiculous. A child, more in attitude than in age."

"I was born just a few—"

"That isn't what I am speaking about. You could have enjoyed that visit, but you chose not to. Your choices are juvenile." A brief pause. "If you are still pouting about your name, get out of your head. Do something to earn one."

She turns away before I can ask what she means.

12
Eagle Eye

AT THE end of my first week in the habitat, we get an unexpected treat. Both Halle and Mussab come to deliver supper. Halle swaps old water bowls for clean ones, while Mussab sets out fresh bowls of food.

"Halle," Mussab mumbles, scuffing his shoes on the ground. "What are you doing tonight?"

"Nothing special."

"Would you... Do you like... How about a coffee?" Mussab asks.

"I don't drink coffee." Halle makes a face. "Can't stand the taste."

Mussab's face falls. "Oh."

"You can buy me a tea, though."

Mussab brightens. "Alright."

They leave our cage in a hurry, almost forgetting to take their supplies with them. Mussab closes the door while his eyes are on Halle. The door bounces back from the latch. They keep walking.

Seize the moment, Sage had told me.

Alright, I will.

As the moon and sun swap places, and the quiet part of the day settles in, I creep toward the door. I nudge it with my torso. It creaks, moving a sliver.

"What are you doing?" Thomas calls. "Escaping?"

"Exploring," I correct.

"Why?" Thomas asks.

"Where?" Herbert pipes up.

I pause. Herbert, the owl I least expect to follow me, strolls over. He gives the door a bump, blinking wildly as it creaks loudly and opens further.

As Thomas gapes at us, we shuffle through.

A few steps away from our pen, we hold still, assessing our options. Behind us, Thomas mutters, "Foolish."

I look at Sage's cage to see if she is near. It takes a moment to find her bold eyes, which are locked on our position. If she disapproves, I can't see it in her expression. She watches us carefully, though, tracking our movements as we hesitantly creep forward.

Once the initial fear evaporates and excitement sets in, I take off running and flap my wings hard. I'm in the air before I realize what I'm doing. The rush of air under my body tingles. I test my abilities, swooping and flying higher and quicker than before. Fear mixes with exhilaration. The moment is brief, yet unforgettable. I wonder if it will feel like this every time.

After a quick twist, I catch sight of Herbert below, motionless and watching. He cannot imitate my actions.

Shame and guilt wash through me. I land, bumping my talons as I do so.

"Excellent flight." There is no trace of jealousy in Herbert's words. I realize then that Herbert accepts what is and what is not, without contempt.

In his shoes, I doubt I would be so noble. Panting, I ask, "Where should we go?"

He glances down the gravel path that humans tread. The west side leads to Sage's cage, and beyond. The east side leads to Hazel and Basil's. I expect him to choose one of these directions. Instead, he nods at the tall wooden fence across from us, the one with netting overhead. "There."

"What's inside?" I ask. Recalling earlier noises, I amend, "Who?"

"I don't know. Never seen them. Are you curious?"

"Yes."

"I can take a peek, then—"

"No. I'll come."

Alright. We set off, legs taking us. Anticipation hastens my stride.

The door is closed, but I remember seeing it swing inward. I lean against it. At first it doesn't budge. Once Herbert adds his strength to mine, it finally thrusts open. Cautiously, we enter the foreign domain.

The grass is lush. A slim path threads through the space, winding in a figure eight. Above, mesh acts as a roof, the stars illuminating faint clouds as they drift by.

Six pairs of eyes shine in the darkness, burrowing into me. In the shadows, I can barely make out three enormous birds of prey.

They are not owls. I believe they are eagles.

One of them steps forward, towering over me. It is shielded by dark-brown feathers. The tip of its tail has dabs of grey, and its nape has a smattering of gold. Its head swings my direction. Blinking, a feminine voice coos, "Hello." There is neither surprise nor alarm in her expression.

The eagle next to her, slightly smaller, turns our way. A jagged scar on his yellow beak moves as he speaks. "Juveniles," he mutters before glancing away.

The first eagle continues to stare at us. "Why have a pair of Great Horned strolled our way?" Immediately, she adds, "*How* have they?"

"Walk and fly, just like every other bird," I say. I regret the sass in my tone immediately.

"That is a simple answer. My name is Stella. The short grump next to me is Hurk."

Hurk grunts, raising a talon to scratch his scarred beak. "You didn't answer Stella's first question. Why are you here?"

Opportunity? An urge? A challenge? I'm not certain of the answer.

"Searching for something?" another voice booms.

Its thick texture adds danger to the words, causing me to shiver. I don't respond aloud, but I *am* searching for something. A name. That likely won't be found here. This is a place with names for others.

The new voice continues, "Searching for something to *steal*?"

Herbert quakes and takes a step closer to me.

Another bird tiptoes from the shadows, similar in size to Stella and Hurk, though far more intimidating. I face the new eagle, my heart tripping. A hooked beak points directly at me. White plumage surrounds eyes that attempt to pierce my skin. Dark brown and black feathers cover its body. Though its movements are slow, they are deliberate. I sense hidden capabilities. I try not to stare at his talons, which are far larger and stronger than mine.

"H-hello," I stammer, voice betraying my alarm.

"Nest thieves."

Stella chirps. "Oh, Rave. Don't start."

Rave unfolds his wings into a massive span.

Herbert steps back. I remain where I am, though my insides tremble.

"Nest thieves." Rave leans forward. "Vermin. Imitators. Commandeers."

Hey! "I—"

"Don't speak, thief!" Rave snaps his beak.

I shiver.

"This young owl is no thief," Stella admonishes.

Rave spins to Stella as soon as the words leave her mouth. "His *kind* are. The Great Horned ones. Instead of building nests, they steal those of others."

"Only some do," Hurk pipes up.

"Enough do," Rave hisses. He glares at Herbert and me without blinking.

"My parents never..." I stop to steady my voice. "We lived in the branches of a tree, with a natural hollow."

Rave pins Herbert with his powerful gaze. "And you?"

Herbert quivers. "I-I-I don't know. A nest."

"Who built it?" Rave demands.

"I don't know." Herbert looks to me. "It was built before I was born."

"So, it could have been stolen from a mighty eagle, seized without warning, or right?" Rave lunges forward.

Stella's calm voice returns. "Rave, these owls are not responsible for the deeds of their parents."

"Possible deeds," I whisper.

Stella speaks over me. "I wouldn't challenge them, either. You know that Great Horned Owls are an even match for eagles such as you or me." There is a trace of caution in her tone.

Rave shakes his head. "These are infants, not adults."

"Juveniles," I correct. Why can't I keep my beak shut?

"I should smother them now, so they won't grow to age," Rave snarls. "Then they can't steal the work of mighty eagles."

Stella shakes her head. "No, you shouldn't."

Suddenly, Rave backs away. Retreating to the shadows, his voice trails to a hiss. "No. Better to pick a lock and teach them a lesson."

A lesson?

Herbert nudges me. "Let's go."

My pounding heart tells me to flee. My wings itch to fly. Or I could run.

I do neither.

"Come on!" Herbert turns and scurries along the ground, darting away from the space of pillars and nets. He pauses in the entryway, his beak clacking incessantly. When I still do not follow, he bolts away in a desperate waddle.

"Your friend is wise," Rave says, out of the shadows once more.

"You said you'd teach us a lesson. What's the lesson?" I dare to ask.

"Perhaps I will steal something of *yours*, nest thieves."

I cock my head. "I have nothing to steal."

"You have friends."

I blink. I think. "Herbert and Thomas?"

"Maybe later. They'd make a full meal. But you have other companions who'll be ideal for a snack. I'll start with them."

"You—? What?"

"I am finished talking." Rave retreats to the shadows again.

I look to Stella. My disbelief is so strong, I can barely blink.

"He hates all Great Horned Owls," she says.

Yes. I'd gathered that.

"He's an odd one," she continues. "Not all eagles are like him. But he's lived a long life. Scars on the inside never healed. All of us here have lost family. Most of us have coped. Others are like Rave."

My nod is false. I do not understand. And also... I do.

"He's confined to this place, just as we are. I wouldn't worry."

My breathing becomes easier. "Thanks, Stella."

Before I turn to go, Hurk adds his two cents. "From his post, Rave can see inside only one cage. When the door is ajar, can you guess who he sees?"

I can't. My mind is paralyzed with fear. My feathers rustle.

Hurk swallows. Though his beak opens, he fails to say more. Stella averts her eyes. She offers no more words of reassurance.

It is my turn to retreat. I back away.

Once free from the eagle den, my breath returns. My brain begins to work again, sorting through details quickly.

Rave's threat echoes through my ears. He wants to eat my friends! But which ones did he threaten?

I glance at my cage, where Herbert is already tucked safely inside. Turning back to the open door of the Eagle's habitat, I realize Rave cannot see him or Thomas. He cannot see Sage from his habitat either. But when I stand in front of Hazel and Basil's pen, the eagle's silhouettes are clearly visible.

That means Rave has a clear view of the Burrowing Owls too.

My wings stiffen.

From the eagle's area, Stella pins her gaze on me. She nods, understanding my fear, her expression forlorn. Hazel and Basil are in danger.

Fearful, I return to my own place.

13

Demonstrations

"AND THEN Rave called us nest thieves," Herbert tells Thomas. "Vermin. Commanders."

"Command*eers*," I correct.

"What's a commandeer?" Thomas asks.

Beaks open, we stared at each other, expressions blank.

Herbert raises his wings an inch, then lowers them. "Whatever it means, it isn't nice," he decides.

Sage listens from her vantage point, her eyes searching for details.

"The eagle tried to run at us," Herbert says, taking a few steps back and then lunging. "He tried to swipe at us with his talons."

Did he? Herbert's version grows more exaggerated every time he tells the story. As if the actual event wasn't scary enough! I can't escape the memory, nor the menacing feeling.

Rave threatened to *steal* my friends, the ones he can see from his cage. The only friends he can see from his cage are Hazel and Basil. Herbert does not relay the threat against the Burrowing Owls. He did not witness it, and I have no desire to share it. I certainly don't want to tell him that Rave has the ability to enter their habitat. How would such a threat affect Hazel and Basil? If I were in their position, would I want the information?

I can't decide.

Butterflies churn in my belly. If I hadn't explored the eagles' pen, the threat would not have been made. My friends are in danger because of me.

As history has already shown, I make poor choices.

"Want to play Run the Fence?"

I snap to attention. Hazel smiles at me expectantly.

I should say *no*. Guilt makes me agree. I race up and down the line of our shared border, dodging branches, weeds, and pebbles. Despite my longer stride, Hazel wins every time.

This is not an accident. I slow my speed on purpose.

Days pass. Visitors come and go, chattering gaily, pointing their rectangles. Mussab and Halle sprint about, fielding questions. With people to observe, hours move swiftly, but time is oddly flipped. Days are too loud, evenings too quiet. All night I listen closely, my gaze pinned across the way, making sure the eagles remain in place.

They do.

Eventually, the tension leaves my body.

All is safe.

ONE BRIGHT summer morning, hours before we usually see him, Mussab strolls by. He wears a special glove on his right hand. Stella perches on his fingers with cords wrapped around her talons. The cords are tucked into Mussab's fist. Stella holds her chest out, her eyes darting about. When she notices us, she offers a regal bow.

"What is happening?" I blurt. "Where is she going?"

Basil pops from a hole in the ground, a narrow one formed by a gopher long ago. "Yay!"

"Yay?" I echo. Panic causes my wings to tremble. Why are the eagles loose?

"It's flight demo day." Hazel strolls close.

"What's that?"

Basil giggles. "It's self-explanatory."

"No, it isn't!" I shriek.

Thomas flies to my perch. "Calm down."

I won't. Can't. I choke out the words, "I... it's... someone, please—"

A loud whistle interrupts my stutter. Halle's voice follows, somehow amplified and flowing through the air around us. While I cannot see her, her words are clear.

"There's a small stadium nearby," Hazel says. "I saw it once. People gather there to see the birds of prey in action."

I nod, her words sinking in slowly.

Halle's disembodied voice continues to fill the air. "Stella here is a Golden Eagle, North America's largest bird of prey. Did you know she can fly at speeds of over 150 miles per hour? How old do you think she is?"

There are murmurs from the crowd.

The mic crackles as Halle continues. "Actually, Stella is seven years old and has been raised in captivity since being found as a baby. We don't know what caused her to be alone so young without her parents, but she has thrived here. While Stella could have returned to the wild, as our program intends with all healthy birds, she has become attached to Hurk, whom she met here. Since Golden Eagles mate for life, and Hurk's injuries prevent him from safe survival in the wild, the pair remain here. Stella is loyal! She refuses to leave her man."

The crowd chuckles. I don't understand why.

"Should we see her fly?" Halle's question is greeted with a small cheer. "Awesome. Stella is smart. All birds of prey conserve their energy. You'll notice she won't leave Mussab's grip until she sees the food I offer. Here she comes." There is a smattering of applause. "You'll note she flies low to the ground and doesn't flap her wings. Again, this is so she doesn't waste her energy."

"These demonstrations happen regularly?" I ask.

The Burrowing Owls *tsk tsk* at me and move away to hear better. I cast my question out again, glancing about. Thomas and Herbert blink at me. They know as little as I do.

There's a rustle in the cage beside me. I turn. Sage peers at me.

"For the bulk of the habitat season, yes, these demonstrations happen regularly," Sage replies. "They don't happen as frequently during the first week, as the crowds are slight. Expect one a day."

"Is it always with Stella?"

"Often. Sometimes hawks and falcons are used. You haven't seen much of the facility. There are many types of birds here. I used to be part of the flight demonstrations before age caught up with me."

"What about the eagles? Is it only Stella?"

"Others participate too, yes. Not Hurk."

"Who else?" I press. "What are their names?"

"What's a name?" Sage counters. "Is that all that matters in this world?"

Right now, yes.

"Rave!" The word bursts forth from my beak. "Do they ever use Rave?"

Silence follows. Long. Deep.

Eventually Sage inhales and responds. "Yes."

I barely breathe. "Why?"

Sage tilts her head. "Rave is an emblem, a ticket to draw crowds. He—"

"What are you talking about?" The words escape as a shriek.

Hazel and Basil turn my way. Herbert jumps. Thomas gapes.

"I'm explaining—" Sage begins.

"No! You never explain anything. You twist riddles and taunt with clues. Can't you speak plainly for once?"

Sage's eyes pierce into me. She holds still for several seconds, then slowly turns her head away. The conversation is over.

Hazel and Basil return to their burrows. Herbert and Thomas avoid me as best they can in our shared space.

My company is misery.

14

Regiment

FOR SEVERAL days, the temperature is scorching hot, forcing us to seek shade. I spend my time wishing for a breeze. The cool evenings are a relief.

Sort of.

At night, I prowl, alert to all sights and sounds, hovering close to the Burrowing Owls' den. Eating is a chore, as my stomach is twisted in knots. Only at dawn can I relax, finding a few hours sleep, aware that daily crowds prevent Rave from following through on his intentions.

My alertness returns each afternoon during the flight demonstrations. Just before, actually, while I wait to see who will parade by on Mussab's arm. Usually, it is Stella. Occasionally, it is one of the eagles I haven't met. Some hawks. A falcon. No owls, though. We are too young.

I work through various scenarios. Hazel answers questions about the depth of their burrows, and how quickly they can access them. The responses leave me unsatisfied, as I don't know how quickly a Bald Eagle can attack. I'm not certain what Rave can do, and what he cannot.

Can he capture the the Burrowing Owls before they find their burrows? Can they escape his talons?

I'm worried for my friends.

I push against the door some nights, hoping it will give. It never does. Though I'm not sure I would be brave enough to saunter back to the eagles, options would be nice. Perhaps I could find more answers and determine if Rave intends to carry through on his threat. I feel trapped. My beak clacks incessantly. My wings flap, taking me nowhere. The action does little to ease my frustration.

My soft down feathers shed in large quantities. Is this normal?

Five days pass. Nothing happens. Rave doesn't appear. Maybe his threat was meaningless. Was he just trying to torture me with words? If so, it worked.

Just when the tension begins to ease, Mussab strolls past wearing his special gloves. He heads into the birds of prey habitat.

When he returns, Rave is perched on his arm.

My stomach flips.

As the pair stroll past, Rave twists his head, his pale-yellow eyes locking on mine, holding my gaze.

My feathers cling tightly to my body. Despite the warmth of the day, a chill surges through me.

A crowd of people follow Mussab and Rave at a safe distance. I wish I could do the same. I want to see what Rave will do. What he can do.

I fly to a high branch to listen, shushing my companions when they offer a comment.

"This is Rave," Halle announces.

I latch onto Halle's voice, my talons coiled tightly.

"Rave is a Bald Eagle, but as you can see, he is not bald at all. The feathers on his head are white, while the rest of him is dark. His wings are broad and rounded, unlike those of a falcon. Did you know his wingspan is nearly two metres wide? That's pretty incredible. Shall we watch him fly?" She grunts. "There he goes!"

Two metres wide?

"Now, as we continue, you'll notice there's a bit of hesitancy between each flight. Rave will only fly when he must. He wants to conserve energy. Unless he sees food, he isn't going to move. As his belly fills, he's less motivated to move." Halle chuckles as she says, "Isn't that true of us all?"

The crowd laughs.

"I think he's got a few more passes in him, though. I'll just dangle this meat ... and he's off!"

This demonstration feels so much longer than the previous ones. I want it to end. I want Rave back where he belongs, locked in his own enclosure and away from my friends.

An odd chill ripples through my feathers. Glancing over my shoulder, I find Sage studying me. Shifting slightly, I give her my back.

Halle's microphone crackles. "Sometimes I think Rave likes to show off. These birds really are a marvel. Remember that your donations help keep birds like him fed and cared for until they are ready for release back into the wild. Rave has been with us for a while, domesticated, so you can visit him anytime, but our goal for as many birds as possible is to send them—"

There's a pause. Some shuffling. "Rave, what are you doing?"

My feathers threaten to burst off my skin. What? What is Rave doing?

Halle giggles nervously.

Mussab voice cuts in. "Don't worry, folks. Rave has decided he's done flying and eating for today. I would have preferred he found his final perch on my glove, but he's completely safe in that tree."

My wings tremble with fear. "If Rave wanted to return to the wild, he could, right now. Not sure that's his goal, though. Guess he just wants to enjoy the view. He's motivated by his stomach, after all, and we have the food. He'll return tonight or tomorrow."

"Has this ever happened before?" someone in the crowd asks.

"A few years ago," Mussab replies. "An owl named Sage. She used to be a regular for our demonstrations. One day, she flew off to a branch and settled there for a week."

Immediately, my head swings toward Sage. She looks away, then shimmies behind the leaves.

"If you want to follow me," Mussab says to the crowd, "I'll take you to tour our owls. Sage is there, as well as a few Great Horneds that will be reintroduced into the wild in a month or two... What's that?... Yes. I can answer your questions about what makes an animal able to return to its natural environment or not. The decision is made by all of us here, though Dr. Millican, our resident vet, has the most influence. Don't worry about Rave. Halle will monitor him and try enticing him to leave his roost. If not, he'll have some freedom to enjoy. It's not a concern."

Not for them, maybe!

All my concerns tumble together in a sickening swirl, and my vision narrows. My surroundings blur, and I flutter to the ground in a feathery heap.

15

Rave

I REGAIN my senses after my fall, but I do not recover. Rave is still out there.

The crowds have dispersed for the day. Meals are delivered, water dishes rinsed. Mussab and Halle finish their final chores and double-check cage locks.

Perhaps they know about the adventure Herbert and I had.

Meanwhile, Hazel and Basil chase each other over and around mounds. Though I call for them, I fail to catch their attention.

How do I make them understand that they need to hide? Escape. Something! What they are capable of is as much a mystery as Rave's intentions. If he comes...

I fear what will happen.

Sage studies me. Her eyes relay that she senses my agitation.

Thomas and Herbert doze, unruffled.

I pace and watch, poised and ready. But ready for what?

Night descends and the Burrowing Owls settle, snuggled together. All is still.

Until it isn't.

A whoosh and a gentle tap announce Rave's landing on the path outside our habitat as much as his presence does. His haunted eyes shine bright against the darkness, searching for me.

Our gazes meet. I become smaller. Less. I am nobody. Small and insignificant. Nameless. Who am I to stand up to a fierce eagle?

Rave gives me a once-over, then turns away. He edges toward the pen of the Burrowing Owls. If they notice his presence, they give no sign.

I fill my lungs. *Screech!*

Herbert and Thomas jump.

"What?" Herbert exclaims.

"Haz-Bas..." I struggle to find words. "Danger!"

"Where? What?" There is no alarm in Thomas' voice.

"Rave."

Herbert shudders. "Thomas, Rave is not a nice bird."

Flapping his wings, though holding fast to his branch, Thomas seeks out Rave. Spying him on the path, he settles. "He's out there. We're fine in here."

"But *they* aren't fine," I say. "Hazel and Basil."

"Why would he harass them?" Herbert asks.

"They're safe where they are too, tucked inside their habitat," Thomas notes.

Unless Rave decides otherwise. This is no time for discussion. This is a time for action. Turning my back on my friends, I dart to the eastern edge of the cage, pressing my body against the wire separating me from Hazel and Basil.

Rave pecks noisily at the lock on their habitat, and they awaken. Wide-eyed, they stare at the predator fighting his way in.

"It's okay," I tell them. "You're alright."

"Says you," Basil quips. "I have a feeling—"

Hazel interrupts, "Why is Rave after us?"

"Ask your friend," Rave rasps, looking up from his work. "He knows."

Basil's head snaps my direction. "What did you do?"

"Nothing! I-I-I met him. He called me a nest thief."

"You *are* a nest thief," Rave tells me. "Your kind all are."

"I'm not—" Convincing him would take too long. Better that I resort to wiser actions. "Hide," I tell my friends.

They flee to separate burrows. Only their heads face out. Their blinking eyes glitter in the darkness.

Rave continues to peck at the latch, raising a talon to aid the process. The lock moves.

I whirl, heading to my own door. Imitating Rave's actions, I pry and stab at its lock with my beak. I cannot raise my leg high enough to use my talons.

"Hurry," Thomas murmurs from above.

As I continue pecking at my lock, the clink of moving metal tells me Rave is close to succeeding. Concentrating

on manoeuvring my beak as best I can, I fight until the spring pops open. I back away, gaping at the twisted latch.

I did it!

"Go," Sage urges.

Pressing my body against the frame, I wedge the door open and wiggle through. A quick flap, and I soar toward the path.

Rave stands in front of the open gate to the Burrowing Owls' habitat, facing me.

Waiting.

Swallowing, I take another step.

16

Confrontation

MY VOICE shakes as I address Rave. "Leave them alone."

The door to Hazel and Basil's sanctuary slams shut. "Alright."

"Alright?" I blink. I flick my gaze left and right, surprised.

"Why would I harm two owls whom I have no problem with?" he asks, stalking forward.

A good question. As Rave nears, I fight to hide my trembling. I will my legs to hold. "So, then...?"

"Who are you?" he demands, hovering above me.

I have to crane my neck to meet his gaze, something I'm not happy to do. His gaze slices into me. My insides quiver.

"I'm... *I'm*..." Is there an answer to this? Who am I? A young, scared Great Horned Owl who is out of his depth, facing situations he's never conceived of, let alone rehearsed.

"What is your name?" Rave demands.

"Uh—"

Rave moves closer. My heart stops for a moment, then beats wildly. My beak would clack if it weren't frozen in fear like the rest of me.

"Why won't you give it? What pride keeps it from others?" Tapping his talons, he spreads his wings wide, a dominating presence.

"I'm not certain I have one."

Rave scoffs. "Everyone has a name."

"Then I don't know what mine is."

"You lie."

"I don't."

"What is your name?" he repeats.

"Why do you want it?" I counter, the words surprising both of us.

Suddenly, Rave backs away. He moves just far enough that I can lower my head to a more comfortable position while still meeting his gaze. His wings relax against his frame.

"I want to know who is cunning enough to escape his pen. Twice. I want to know the name of one who is not afraid of walking among birds older and larger than himself."

Oh, I *was* daunted. Incredibly so. "I'm . . . *me*."

"Me? What an unusual name."

"No, I—" I swallow. My brain spins. "It's . . . my name . . . is usual."

"Really?"

"My father shares it." The lie slips out easily.

"Interesting." He gazes to his left. "Me."

The softest of noises stirs behind me. Rave's attention snaps toward it. I glance over my shoulder, discovering Sage.

"What is your interest in this matter, Great Grey?" Rave hisses.

"For now, to observe," Sage replies.

"There is nothing to watch," Rave declares.

"Then I will absorb the silence. Appreciate the stillness," Sage states calmly.

Rave releases another hiss. "Leave."

"No." There is power in the simplicity of Sage's rejection.

I'm caught between the pair. They're different species, yet alike in other ways. Elders. Full of depth, wisdom, experience.

"This is between me and the youngling," Rave insists.

"The youngling you accused of being a nest thief?" Before either of us could question how Sage knew that, she adds, "I know because I listen. Observe mannerisms. Watch the threads of the day unfold."

Rave's feathers ruffle. "You speak in riddles."

"I speak truth. This owl is no nest thief. If his parents were, your cause is with them. If any owl has stolen what was yours, then words can solve that issue, not violence, so lower your talons."

I whirl, catching Rave's movement as he withdraws the talon hovering at my back. I squeak in surprise and shuffle closer to Sage. She nods at me.

"You have regrets in your life, Rave. That is acceptable. Placing these regrets on another's plate is not." Sage takes one step and stands beside me. She raises a wing, and I huddle under it. I feel protected. Memories of my parents' comfort and affection flow through me.

"Do you miss your family?" I ask Rave.

"No one asks me that," he replies.

That's not an answer. "Do you miss your family?"

"I miss many things."

"It's okay to grieve," I tell him.

He dips his head. Though he looks at me, he directs his words to Sage. "You have a protégé, it seems. One as wise as you are. Someone to guide those who are lost. To offer wisdom and assurance. The owls are lucky."

"The eagles, too," I state.

Rave tilts his head. "How so?"

"They have you. You can defend and protect them. Share your knowledge."

Rave takes flight, his massive wings extended. There's beauty to the image, the action. I wonder if that's how I appear when I fly.

He soars high, then swoops low, landing just outside the door to the eagle's sanctuary. Following the barest of backward glances, he disappears.

17

Advice

SAGE ESCORTS me to her pen instead of mine. I duck my head to evade the questioning glances of Thomas and Herbert as they stare our way, beaks agape.

When Sage halts, I do too. There's a moment where she simply breathes, inhaling deeply and purposefully. I think she is listening, absorbing the atmosphere, as she claims to do. I do the same, waiting for her to interrupt the silence.

"Do you still seek a name?" she finally asks.

I'm afraid to answer. To tell her the truth.

Sage glances down at me. "You've done so much without one."

"I don't think so. You were the one who protected me against Rave."

"Did I?" Sage returns her gaze to the sky. "I believe you protected yourself. You have abilities beyond what you perceive. Who snuck to the eagles' pen to begin with? Conversed with them. Acted as an equal, despite your

age. You were the one who sought to protect smaller owls. Your determination made it possible to undo the lock."

"But I was just—"

For the first time since meeting her, Sage speaks quickly, overtop my words. "You spoke through fear, using words to solve a quarrel. This maturity, this courage, you own without a name."

My voice is small as I say, "It would still be nice to have one."

"Fair enough. So, select one."

"What if...?" I begin.

Sage waits for me to gather my thoughts.

Finally, I ask, "What if it isn't the right one?"

"What is a 'right' name?"

"I mean, what if it doesn't fit?"

"A name doesn't define you. A name just *is*. It's as much a part of you as your wing. Think of Herbert."

"Herbert?"

She doesn't elaborate, expecting me to understand. "If you grow, inside or out, and find your name doesn't match anymore, you can change it. Adopt another or select multiple."

"I can do that?"

"You, little owl, can do so much."

The conversation ends there. As silence stretches on, Sage remains still. Feeling that I'm trespassing on her sanctuary, I head back for my own habitat. There, I field anxious questions from Herbert and Thomas, and push away words of gratitude from Basil and Hazel.

Sleep is a long way off.

I FIND myself staring at Herbert the next day for long stretches, pondering Sage's words: *A name just is. It's a part of you, as much as your wing is. Think of Herbert.* What did she mean by that? It takes hours before I understand that my fellow Great Horned Owl remains who he is with or without an injured wing. There is more to him than this one part. The same is true of Hurk with his outer scars or Rave with his hidden ones.

A name will not change me. It cannot take away, but simply add dimension to who I already am.

I can choose a name. I don't yet know what it might be. There is no rush.

The decision makes me feel lighter.

18

Home

THE SEASON passes by, the heat intense. People mostly visit in the morning and late afternoon, avoiding the hottest part of the day. Flight demonstrations continue as usual, with Stella, the regular attraction, and Rave, the occasional star. There are no more unexpected flight paths from the resident Bald Eagle. When he passes by, he gives a regal nod to Sage and a short one to me. He chooses not to speak.

I grow. My downy feathers are replaced by thicker, darker coverings. My muscles become stronger, and my vision improves. I can see more. I know more. Experience as much as time has led me to age.

The air changes, and leaves begin a slow descent from trees. A mild frost tinges the morning air. Winds grow more abrupt. Sharing memories of our families, Thomas, Herbert, and I snuggle close when chilled. We allow ourselves to embrace sadness, longing, and even loneliness.

Flight demonstrations cease. Crowds of visitors minimize and then fade away completely. One day, as Halle removes Sage from her habitat, she murmurs soft words about finding warmer accommodations.

I'm unable to share parting words, as is Sage. I stare at her empty pen for hours until Thomas asks, "You alright?"

Blinking, I say, "I miss Sage."

"Understandable." Thomas flits away.

A few more days pass. Long ones, full of dullness. Then Mussab arrives wearing those special gloves. First, he grabs Thomas, who is stunned to stillness. Holding Thomas's legs firmly, Mussab lifts him in the air, carries him from the habitat, and places him on the path outside.

Then Mussab comes for me. I take flight, but the human is quick. When I land on the nearest branch, he seizes me, pinning my legs like he did with Thomas. Like the Christopher once did.

I'm placed on the pathway outside my habitat, next to Thomas—the very place my encounter with Rave happened. Memories flood over me until uncertainty about my current situation washes them away.

Mussab watches expectantly.

What is happening?

I have never been outside my cage with humans observing. Doing so in daylight feels strange as well. The freeness of the outdoors is unusual. I gaze at the open sky. Despite puffs of clouds, the blueness strikes me. No wire blocks my view.

Thomas sidles close, whispering, "Are we supposed to be doing something?"

"I don't know."

Dr. Millican arrives. He crouches down and observes us for several minutes. Then he lifts Thomas by caging his feet and proceeds with an examination. He raises Thomas's wings and scratches his head. Then it is my turn. My beak doesn't clack. I'm not nervous. Just confused.

Very.

When Dr. Millican places me down, he turns to Mussab. "I think it's time."

Time for what?

He brings in two boxes similar to the one I first arrived in. A blanket lines each. Thomas is placed in one, me in the other. We could fly out but neither of us does. I've trusted these people until now. Besides, staying with Thomas seems wise.

Halle rushes over. She peeks into Thomas's box, then mine. "You weren't going to leave without saying goodbye, were you?" She turns to Dr. Millican. "Where are they off to?"

"Home," he replies. "I think they are ready."

Home.

Home?

Home!

"Will their families accept them?" Mussab asks.

"I don't know," Dr. Millican replies. "Hopefully. Either way, this pair is strong. They'll manage to figure it out.

We haven't had a release in a while. It'll be nice to send these two back where they belong."

Halle sobs. "I'll still miss them."

Mussab wraps an arm around her shoulder. "That's allowed."

I feel happy and scared at the same time. Home. Mother. Father. Sister. I can return to normal. Back to who I was.

Or can I? What did Mussab suggest? That our families might reject us?

For a moment, I can't breathe. Panicked, I gaze at Thomas. He looks terrified. His beak clacks incessantly.

"It's okay," I tell him, finding a way to fill my lungs. "Even if our families—"

"My family is gone. That is how I ended up here."

"Oh."

"But what if..." Thomas's eyes grow moist. "What if home isn't the same? What if it doesn't feel right?"

"It won't," I decide. "Because we've changed."

"Do you think we'll be able to feed ourselves? Survive on our own?"

"If we have to." My words hold power. Saying them might make them so. "We've managed so much already. A bit more learning won't matter."

"I suppose," Thomas reflects. "Taught ourselves how to fly, didn't we? Hunting is the next natural step."

"Yes."

"And there will always be other birds out there."

"Great Horneds and Great Greys," I agree. "Burrowing Owls and Golden Eagles. Bald Eagles and falcons and hawks."

"Well, now I'm excited." Thomas's voice vibrates. The clacking stops. "I'm ready for a challenge. Ready for the world."

"Me too," I agree.

Halle lifts my box. Mussab raises the box Thomas is in. We are brought to a familiar truck. Christopher is there, still wearing his yellow hat. "Hey, pal. It's a been a while."

As the truck starts moving, Thomas speaks. "I'd like to say a proper goodbye. Didn't get to do so with Herbert. I was just thinking, though. Did I ever catch your name?"

"No," I say.

"Can I?"

"Why?" I ask.

He startles. "So that when I make new friends and speak of my adventures, I have someone to refer to."

That is a good enough reason for me. "Some call me Snowy," I tell him. "To others, I'm Marble Eyes. Fledgling. Me."

"And what do you call yourself?" Thomas asks.

I could choose a name that sounds pleasant on my tongue, and I might opt for one like that later. Right now, though, I want a name that symbolizes my strength. My ability to endure. A reminder to myself that I am capable of many things, difficult or new.

"Resilience," I tell him. "My name is Resilience."

"I like that name."

Me too. I can't wait to share it with my family. To tell them what I've seen, who I've met, and what I've done.

And who I am.

I think I'm starting to know.

Author's Note

STORY IDEAS can come from anywhere: dreams, memories, sounds, or conversations. *An Owl without a Name* was inspired by a real event.

Eight months after moving to an acreage near Coaldale, Alberta, my husband encountered a young owl while mowing the lawn. The injured creature was stranded on the ground, wing feathers caught in a low wire fence that lined our property. Believing him to be a Snowy Owl because of his white feathers, my husband and daughter named him "Snowy."

A phone call to the Alberta Birds of Prey Centre (burrowingowl.com), which was fifteen minutes away, brought Colin to our home. He untangled Snowy and explained he was actually a young Great Horned Owl, who had likely fallen from his nest. Colin taught us a lot of facts about juvenile owls, before he safely transported Snowy to the Alberta Birds of Prey Centre for rehabilitation. That same summer, we were able to visit Snowy living in a safe habitat with fellow owls.

An Owl without a Name is my invention of how the events of that summer might have unfolded from Snowy's perspective. Although a few details about Snowy's injury, rehabilitation, and the rescue centre are drawn from real life, the story is a work of fiction.

If you find a sick, injured, or orphaned bird or other wild animal, do not touch it or pick it up. Instead, call an accredited wildlife rescue and rehabilitation centre in your area. These organizations will treat injured animals with the aim of releasing them back into the wild once they have recovered. It is important to respect wild animals and protect their natural habitats.

Acknowledgements

I WISH to thank the team at Heritage House Publishing for seeing the potential in this story and making it a reality. I am equally in debt to the editors who helped fine-tune the manuscript: Taija Morgan and Deborah Froese.

Thanks, mom! You made me a storyteller. Dad, you encouraged something you didn't understand, and that is the epitome of good parenting. Aunt Liz, you are both mentor and friend. My dear daughter, you are the inspiration for everything and always will be. This story, and each one yet to come, is for you. Scott, thanks for accepting and loving this "adorkable" mess and giving me gentle nudges to work through edits.

Thank you, Kristy, Rachel, Fleur, Candace, Tammy, Kendra, Jessica, Christi. You are my love and support. Love you, Hailee and Kaitlyn!

Lastly, a large tribute must be sent to the Alberta Birds of Prey Centre for helping birds of prey in need.

About the Author

JENNA GREENE is an author of YA and children's fiction, best known for the award-winning Reborn Marks series, and co-host of the *Jot Notes* podcast, where she interviews authors from all over the world. When not writing or podcasting, she can be found in the classroom, teaching Grades 1 and 2. For more information, visit jennagreene.ca.